*Miracle
in the
Wilderness*

# Books by
# PAUL GALLICO

## Novels

ADVENTURES OF HIRAM HOLLIDAY

THE SECRET FRONT          THE SNOW GOOSE

THE LONELY          THE ABANDONED

TRIAL BY TERROR          THE SMALL MIRACLE

THE FOOLISH IMMORTALS          SNOWFLAKE

LOVE OF SEVEN DOLLS          THOMASINA

MRS. 'ARRIS GOES TO PARIS

LUDMILA          TOO MANY GHOSTS

MRS. 'ARRIS GOES TO NEW YORK

SCRUFFY          CORONATION

LOVE, LET ME NOT HUNGER

THE HAND OF MARY CONSTABLE

MRS. 'ARRIS GOES TO PARLIAMENT

THE MAN WHO WAS MAGIC

THE POSEIDON ADVENTURE

THE ZOO GANG          MATILDA

THE BOY WHO INVENTED THE BUBBLE GUN

MRS. 'ARRIS GOES TO MOSCOW

# Miracle in the the Wilderness

## A Story of Colonial America

## BY
# PAUL GALLICO

DELACORTE PRESS / NEW YORK

Simultaneously published in Great Britain
by William Heinemann Ltd.

Copyright © 1955, 1975
by Paul Gallico and Mathemata Anstalt

Manufactured in the United States of America

Second printing–1976

*Design by Barbara Liman Cohen*

Library of Congress Cataloging in Publication Data

Gallico, Paul, 1897–
Miracle in the wilderness.

I. Title.
PZ3.G13586Md     [PS3513.A413]          813'.5'2
75–16277
ISBN 0–440–05714–0
ISBN 0–440–05715–9 Special

TO
*VIRGINIA*

THIS STORY was told to me when I was a boy, by my great-grandmother on a Christmas Eve by the fire. I always believed that stories told by great-grandmothers must be so, for their old eyes look inward and they recall. Or perhaps when it is something that has happened in the long-ago far beyond their lifespan or even those of generations preceding them they remember things that someone before them has remembered.

I never knew whether this was something she had heard, or perhaps read in old letters yellowing in an attic, but only that it happened in the wilderness of Britain's colony in the New World, in the long distant past on Christmas Eve.

Time had diminished my great-grandmother to the weightlessness of a bird and as fragile, yet her dark eyes were bright with communication and undiminished life. At ninety she was as hale and active seemingly as ever she had been. As she spoke, glowing pictures formed themselves in my mind for she had the storyteller's gift, punctuating her narrative with alert and vigorous gestures.

Hers was the power to cause me to hear sounds out of the past and even as she would wrinkle her tiny, almost translucent nose I would capture a whiff of long forgotten odors.

The parlor where we forgathered was warmed by the log fire and filled with the pine and sugar scented fragrance of the Christmas tree but time and place were banished as she spoke. Her voice, when she began, was crisp and dry like the crunch of snowshoes on the feet of the Indian scouts she told about. It was as though she had known them intimately, rasping over the hard crust of week old snow in the dark forest of

the wilderness as they made their way northwards by a last quarter moon with their three
captives, the man, the woman and the infant.

She made me see the file proceeding along
the beaten forest trail where the moonlight
breaking through the treetops cast blue shadows on the surface and distorted the forms
of the Algonkin raiding party, hulking in
their furs of beaver and muskrat, causing
them to loom more huge and monstrous even
than they were. She helped me to smell the
rancid fetor of the Indians against the crisp-
ness of frost on spruce and pine, the leathery
odor of buckskin and the rich animal hair of
the pelts they wore against the cold.

Occasionally there was the thunder of a slip of snow disturbed from a laden branch, from time to time the clash of a steel axe-head against musket butt, the snort or explosive exhalations of the pony of the mounted Indian and the heartbreaking moans of the woman who had been roughly handled. The Indians did not try to maintain silence for it was impossible in the winter forest. They relied upon swiftness to take them out of reach of any pursuing parties of Iroquois bent on rescue or vengeance.

Darker than the forest aisles was the agony of mind of Jasper Adams because of the disaster that had overtaken them this morning of December 24, 1755, and his knowledge of the fate that awaited them when they reached Algonkin territory. More poignant still was the anguish and torment of his wife Dorcas who, through a moment's heedlessness and disobedience, had been the unwitting cause of the catastrophe.

The land where Jasper Adams had settled, cleared the forest and built the cabin that was about half stout fort and where Dorcas was delivered of Asher, their first born, was hewed out of the northwest section of New York, not far from French-controlled territory.

Though roughly protected by a chain of

British posts, they depended rather on the sturdiness of the house and the vigilance and knowledge of Jasper. He had hunted and farmed the frontier for ten years before he married Dorcas Bonner, young, lovely and but newly arrived from England with her family, part of yet another trickle of landless emigrants from the old country hoping to improve their fortunes in the New World. They had reached Albany by schooner. There Dorcas had been wooed and won by Jasper who had journeyed eastward for supplies to maintain his outpost home, tools, plowshares, gunpowder, lead for bullets.

Young wives were at a premium in those

days in the colonies and Dorcas was sought by many brave young men but once she laid eyes on Jasper there was none other for her and for Jasper it was like a dream of having found an angel from heaven. They were wed in Albany in accordance with the rites of their beliefs; they were simple God-fearing people and the sole book tucked away amongst the goods carried by the pack mule was the Bible. Dorcas rode Jasper's farm Percheron. Strong Jasper marched on foot. Thus they moved north and westward through the wilderness in advance of the wave of colonists that was to follow and which, unsettling the French, in the already half-century old struggle for the New World, was turning that nation to a renewed policy of intimidation.

It was unusual for the Algonkin to attack in December, yet that winter the alarming westward spread of the English threatening the Ohio Valley decided the French upon the political necessity of recourse to terrorism to stem the flow and they sent surprise raiding parties burning farms and carrying off captives as hostages or to torture and death to provide cards of diplomacy to be played back and forth across the English Channel.

Now such a party was pushing northward, returning single file through the moonlit woods. Quanta-wa-neh, the leader of the expedition, rode at the head of the procession on a shaggy Indian pony and the rest of the party with the captives in the center, surrounded by some dozen warriors bundled in furs and blankets, marched on foot. At Quanta's side trudged fat Nyagway, the Seneca renegade who spoke English. Quanta had thrown out scouts on snowshoes to the side and rear against any sudden surprise ambush. Nevertheless, he was uneasy. The speed of his retreat was limited by the capacity of the captives.

One of the raiders carried the eight-month-old child Asher over his shoulder wrapped in a blanket from whence its head emerged every so often to gaze about—silent, solemn, interested, unafraid.

Close behind, the mother followed, her dark eyes rarely leaving the bundle over the Algonkin's back except for an occasional fearful glance at the craggy features and deep lines seaming the countenance of her stern, tall husband who limped and sometimes staggered beside her, his hands bound behind his back with buckskin thongs. She stumbled along the trail in shock from the calamity and the manhandling to which she had been subjected, close to the point of exhaustion, ameliorated only by the occasional rest periods.

The procession came to a halt for a moment and Nyagway, the Seneca interpreter, obese, short of breath and waddling like a bear, came down from the head of the line. Peering with beady eyes out of a cloak of muskrat fur he looked more Eskimo than Indian. He spoke to Jasper Adams: "Quanta say you go faster or you, woman and young one die now."

Jasper glanced at Nyagway out of eyes glazed with pain and nodded. "I will try." Then he uttered aloud a prayer: "Oh Lord! Thou art my staff and support in time of need. Give me the strength."

Nyagway regarded the white man for an

instant but without hostility and then shuf-
fled unhappily back to his position. He was
too old and adipose for this sort of work. A
vain and lazy man, he had originally defected
to the Algonkin in the hope that his knowledge of English would prove useful to the
French and bring him a sinecure. Instead, the
northern tribe, with contempt for the turn-
coat, used him on missions involving long
and arduous journeys.

Forcing himself to renewed effort, Jasper
quickened his pace and the line moved more
swiftly through the forest to carry out the
cruel and horrid paradox the Indians had set
their prisoners: march quicker lest you die

now so that you may the faster reach the place where you will die then.

The fearful irony of the command and their situation was plain to Jasper and for a moment anger stabbed him as he thought of his wife's foolish disregard of his order never to leave the door of the cabin unbarred when he was away or out of sight of the house.

But in an instant love replaced anger with immense pity as he read the anguish of maternity reflected in the eyes that rested on her child. It touched his heart how haggard trial had turned the beauty that had been his delight and because of this he loved her the more.

He found the strength to whisper, "It is better so. If we do their bidding they may adopt the child into the tribe and thus he will live." In this manner he tried to comfort her. He blamed himself for their plight. He had had no right to expose someone so young and innocent to such a wild and savage land and the dangers of the wilderness. It had been the proximity of the familiar gentle feast of Christmas and the endearing femininity of Dorcas that had been their undoing.

That bright clear sunny morning Jasper had disappeared into the woods to shoot a turkey for their dinner and again admonished her to caution. She had watched him cross the clearing and vanish into the forest with a smile of fond indulgence for his endless warnings. They had lived there for over a year now without so much as a sight of a hostile Indian. The Iroquois were friendly and traded with them or carried news or messages.

The day had been so fine, the sun in the cloudless sky so warm, almost like summer in the still air. Dorcas had moved Asher's crib outside the cabin to let the child bask some of the winter pallor from his cheeks. Nearby was the pile of holly, mistletoe and pinecones that Jasper had gathered to decorate their cabin. For tomorrow was Christmas, their first since the new house that Jasper had built was finished and she bethought herself how she might make herself attractive and please her husband on this holy and happy Christmas Day.

On an impulse she had climbed up into the loft where the smoked hams hung with the flitches of bacon, bags of filberts and hickory nuts and bundles of dried herbs and in the corner next to the heap of winter apples she had gone delving into the horsehide box she had brought with her all the way from England and where the treasures of her girlhood were stored.

And there she had been trapped, musing

over a bit of lace and the matching of some silk ribands to go with the red of the holly berries and the white of the mistletoe, when the raiding Algonkin stormed in. With the child already in their hands it was hopeless. She had fought bravely and desperately and had been brutally subdued. The rising column of smoke from their burning home brought Jasper running from the woods and into the ambush. He had not even time to fire his fowling piece before the Indians were upon him and beat him almost into insensibility with their pogamoggans, as their crooked, knob-headed war clubs were called. They had stopped just short of killing him.

Quanta's orders had been to bring in the captives alive—if possible. Now, on the way back, the Indian leader had not expected to be handicapped by a man hardly able to walk.

And so the captives moved onwards through the snowy forest pierced occasionally by the bright night and slowly approached the end of their resources. Only his determination to save the life of his son if he could and the incredible will to survive that animated the men of those days enabled Jasper to continue the pace. And Dorcas, the weaker vessel, faltered now. As the Indians reckoned time they marched for an hour and rested five minutes. It was not sufficient to restore her and she moved like an automaton, following the child, stumbling, and once Jasper heard her murmur as though her mind was wandering and she thought herself safe at home at her fireside.

At the head of the march, Quanta-wa-neh wrestled with the exigencies. Beneath his furs, his paint, feathers, beads and medicine bags, he was a human being beset by most of the problems that have dogged the footsteps of man and leaders down through the ages. In this case it was protection, providing, acquiring and survival, not only for himself but the lives of his command for which he was responsible. He was sometimes savage and ruthlessly cruel as dictated by tribal custom, policy or necessity but he was no more devoted to such cruelty by nature than, say, his white brothers who in their day had plied the rack, hot irons and thumbscrews for the Inquisition. He was an experienced and practical commander.

It was for these traits among others that Quanta-wa-neh had been assigned to the work at hand. A veteran warrior of some forty odd years he was a tall, wiry Indian with a shrewd, not unpleasant countenance, graceful and moving with the quiet assurance of the born leader who knew what he was about.

Now, slowed in passage beyond what he considered the point of safety in spite of the element of surprise he had achieved, he reviewed his position in the light of his military command and his orders to bring in any captives alive if he could. He had no personal interest in the life or death of his prisoners whatsoever.

The taking of hostages was a part of Indian warfare as well as the white man's. If and when they became a nuisance or a menace to the safety of an operation they were simply slain out of hand as a matter of military necessity. He would do what was needed.

The way darkened as they passed beneath

a canopy of giant oaks and conifers that shut out the light from both the moon and the stars. The sobbing of the woman and the whistling breath of the stricken man reached Quanta's ears and brought him to the verge of a decision when they reached an opening in the forest, a kind of circular glade made by some ancient vagary of the wind strewing the acorns so that the trees grew in a circle open to the sky.

Into this glade the moonlight shone and, ringed by the dark shadowy forest, illuminated it like an amphitheater. The shaft, as though streaming from an opening in heaven itself, revealed the most extraordinary sight.

Three white-tailed deer knelt in the snow; a buck, his noble antlers not yet shed, his doe and her fawn, as motionless as statues, their gentle faces turned towards the east.

Quanta heard the swift rustle at his side that told him his lieutenant had plucked an arrow from his quiver, notched it to the bowstring and drawn it to his ear, for here was meat. Yet he held up his arm in warning, came to a halt and whispered, "Stay your hand. For such a thing as this I have never seen before."

Nor had any of the others and for once the Indians were surprised out of their habitual silence as a murmur of astonishment rippled through their ranks and the bowman lowered his weapon muttering, "Look, they do not move. And the fawn, it was born out of season. Is this a magic?"

Yet even more astonishing was the fact that as the party formed a semicircle at the edge of the clearing, the beasts did not take fright but remained motionless in the attitude in which they had been discovered, hind legs erect, their forelegs folded beneath them, all three alike, and in this strange attitude casting a purple shadow upon the snow, their moist muzzles and liquid eyes reflecting moonlight.

The surprise rustled from the leaders down

through the ranks of the Indians and still within sight, sound and scent of the presence of man the three beasts remained immovable and undisturbed as though under some kind of spell of devotion.

Now to Jasper Adams it appeared that beyond the mysterious and unfrightened deer, beneath the branches of a great oak, he saw a glowing and at the center of it there was a primitive cradle such as the one he had constructed for Asher to sleep in at home. In it lay a swaddled infant and the glowing that surrounded it came neither from the moon nor the stars.

And it seemed to him too that he heard

voices and speech from the beasts of the forest even as the legend had it of the miracles of Christmas Eve and that they were murmuring in unison, "Glory to God in the highest. On earth peace, goodwill toward men."

Then he likewise knelt in the snow crying to his wife, "Ah, Dorcas! Kneel thou too! For it is midnight of the eve of Christmas when Jesus was born and the beasts of burden and the wild things of the field and forest bend the knee to worship and adore Him and are given the power of speech to pray."

Dorcas had taken her child from the Algonkin who was too amazed to resist and cradling it in her arms tightly to her breast she also knelt. Her lips moved but her eyes were blinded by tears.

Then Jasper Adams, with no thought of themselves or their plight, prayed a welcome to The Child, "Gentle Jesus, come to be our Savior. I will worship Thee and hearken to Thy commandments. Glory to God in the highest and on earth peace, goodwill toward men. . . ."

Quanta was mystified and impressed by the strange sight and the agony which he knew the white man must be enduring for he had both dealt the man some of his wounds and performed the rough surgery on

them. Fortitude he could understand and ad-
mire but here undoubtedly was a great mys-
tery. He said to Nyagway, "Ask him does he
know the meaning of this."

Nyagway did so. Jasper Adams replied
only, "Hush! Kneel down, all ye, and pray
likewise. Praise the Lord God on high for
this is the hour of the birth of his only begotten Son."

Confused, the interpreter translated as best
he could and the Indians moved uneasily in
the presence of the unknown. The antlered
buck now heaved himself slowly to his fore-
feet followed by the doe and the little fawn,
but remained yet standing there unafraid on

the carpet of snow in the center of the glade.

To Dorcas, too, it seemed as though there had been a peal of sounds of beauty as though from above and she felt herself suffused with a new courage and a great love and she pressed her child more closely to her breast and loved and wept over him.

For yet another moment the buck remained standing, his head raised high seemingly oblivious to those ringing the edge of the glade and to Jasper Adams his proud penetrating glance appeared to be directed at him, piercing him to the marrow as though communicating a shared experience. Then slowly the beast turned and followed in single file by his doe and fawn trotted across the circle and vanished in the darkness of the forest.

The majestic passage of these lords of the woods had hypnotized the Indians into unbelieving silence so that they were hardly aware of the departure until they looked again and saw that the animals had disappeared as though they had never been there. And yet, although the moonbathed glade was empty there was evidence of the disturbed snow where they had knelt and their tracks leading away.

Quanta with a shudder said to Nyagway, "Ask him what is this magic. To what Manitou does he pray?"

Nyagway translated. Jasper Adams endured the torment of regaining his feet, but Dorcas, lacking the strength, remained in the snow rocking her child.

"To the Lord God and His only begotten Son Jesus Christ who was born on this Holy Night for to save the sinners of the world. . . ."

Quanta was puzzled. "But what of the deer that knelt?" he asked. "Is there a tale?"

Jasper Adams said to Nyagway, "Tell him aye."

Quanta instructed, "Release him. Order him that we would hear it now."

The Indians like children squatted cross-legged, Nyagway in the center, his fat features as placid as a Buddha's as he attuned himself to his task.

Jasper Adams, his hands freed, stood swaying, fighting to hold himself erect, struggling to remember through the fog of pain his Testaments and childhood teachings.

He began: "A new star appeared in the sky over Bethlehem on such a night as this many hundreds of years ago, one never before seen by any man. In the east, Three Wise Men were traveling. They saw the star in the Heavens and knew that the King of All had been born. They turned aside and followed the star to bring Him gifts. And the shepherds in the fields tending their flocks saw the star and heard an angel and came likewise."

The encircling Indians listening to the translation grunted "Heh!" or "Hau!" and settled themselves more comfortably. Bethlehem meant nothing to them but they knew of stars and kings and wise men and the tending of flocks in the field. And also they gathered that this was a tale, like so many of their own, that was of old.

Nyagway, the center of attention, was in his element. His flat features became animated, his small eyes glowed. He gestured and his voice picked up the inflections of Jasper Adams who seemed to gain in strength and joy as he unfolded his story.

"To Bethlehem there came two travelers, Mary and Joseph, husband and wife, and Mary was large with child. But the child was not of Joseph, but of God, for the spirit of God had entered into Mary."

The listeners and even Quanta murmured, "Hau Hau!" and nodded their heads for talk of spirits they could understand.

Dorcas hugged her child and looking upwards saw one whose strength and depth she had not even dreamed. Lover and husband he had been, but now he seemed touched by God as well. He towered so tall that his head reached into the sky, crowned with light, the shadows of his great arms were longer than the dark spreading branches and his voice booming through the forest aisles was like organ music.

"When it came Mary's time there was no place for them at the inn at Bethlehem nor would any humans give them shelter. So they went to a stable and there in the manger the infant Jesus was born. And about His head there was such a glowing as there is in the Heavens tonight."

For much of what Jasper was narrating Nyagway had no point of reference and could not wholly understand. He interpreted it in terms of Indian life, shocking his listeners with the revelation of the lack of hospitality and cruelty of the fact that no one would take in these wayfarers and that the woman had to go to give birth where the beasts were gathered. But when it came to the glow in the heavens they were at home and all followed Nyagway's gesture and looked up into the milky sky behind which apparently were hidden the mysteries of the white man as well as their own. Dorcas gazed into the face of her husband and what she saw was both tender and terrible.

The story continued: "And the ox bowed down to worship and gave the Infant of his soft straw for His bed. And the ass bowed down to worship and gave the Infant of her warm milk to drink. And the sheep too bowed down to worship and crowded close with their soft wool to keep the Infant warm."

Thrice Nyagway bowed as he narrated and his audience swayed in movement with his body.

". . . and ever since that time the beasts of burden and the creatures of the field and forest kneel down in secret at midnight of Christmas Eve. This night, as they did so long ago, they worship the Christ Child and are given the power of human speech to pray to Him."

Quanta's breath was exhaled in a long, hissing sigh. "Ah. The deer!" Then he asked of Nyagway, "Were they then heard to speak? What were their words?"

When the question was put to him Jasper had to listen for a moment within himself for he was not quite certain whether he had heard it or thought it. And then it seemed to him that he heard quite clearly. "They prayed to the Lord God and the Infant Jesus, 'Oh Almighty Father and gentle Jesus, watch over us and protect us from the wolves, from the tree cats, from hunger and thirst and the hunter. Let Thy grace descend upon us so that we may live together in peace and love one another.' "

Quanta nodded. He was himself a family man and the words and imagery pleased him. He asked, "And what became of this child?"

Jasper Adams felt his strength beginning to fail him. Nevertheless he undertook to reply, "His name was Jesus and He grew up to become a great preacher. He preached that God, His Father, was our Father and the Father of all. Those who did not believe in Him or His message caused Him to be tortured and nailed to a cross until He gave up the ghost. He died so that men all over the world would remember the love that He preached. And after the third day He rose from His tomb and joined His Father in

Heaven and men believed and worshiped Him."

Jasper spoke no more. He was close to the end of his resources and would have fallen but for clutching the shoulder of Nyagway who having interpreted the last sentences added, "The tale is at an end. The white man is very ill." The Indians had fallen quite silent and Quanta's head was momentarily sunk upon his chest in some kind of faraway contemplation.

There occurred then a diversion that sent the party springing to its arms as two snow-shoe-equipped Algonkin scouts hurried in from a side trail and conferred with Quanta.

The gist of their report was that a large force of Iroquois with some English was no more than a few hours behind.

Quanta's lieutenant gestured towards the captives. "Shall I kill them?"

Quanta debated. A word, a nod, a flashing of axe blades in the moonlight and he would be relieved of this hazard to the security of his command. He would have concluded the raid to the best of his ability. Yet he hesitated.

Quanta was himself a deeply religious man and where a Christian would have crossed himself, now his fingers sought and touched the little medicine bundle that hung about his neck, a collection of small objects, a queerly shaped stone, some feathers, the leg bone of a small animal and some dried plants, objects endowed with magical properties, talismans wrapped in an otter-skin always carried on his person. He feared and worshiped many mysterious and unseen beings of the forest as well as the manifestations of nature, the skies overhead, lightning, thunder, fire and water and he recognized the mysterious cosmic powers abounding everywhere in his world.

And as he clutched his medicine bag for protection and thought, it came to him that while the beliefs of himself and the people from over the seas were so different one should not be disrespectful towards strange

Gods and the magic of others and that if this were the night of the Great Manitou of the white man to whom even the wild deer bowed down in prayer, it might not be propitious to harm them.

In the specific religion of the Algonkin tribes of the north country their chief deity was a mighty Great Hare who lived behind the sky. How this little animal slipping furtively through the forest paths, shy and elusive, had grown to be their all-encompassing, omnipotent deity, Quanta did not know. Surely it went back to some ancient tale, the beginnings of which had been forgotten even by the wisest and most long-lived of the elders. But as he looked up into the same bright winter canopy behind which his captive had seen his Manitou and Father he visualized spreading from horizon to horizon the softness of the belly of the symbolic animal to which he would be gathered when death finally came to him and in the warmth of whose bosom he would rest in eternal bliss.

For a moment the thought flashed through his mind, the Great Hare and the Father and the Son by the woman who was denied the hospitality of the lodge, were they perhaps one and the same? But then it seemed to him it could not be so, that the tale was too strange and that besides the Great Hare there were other Gods and they must not be offended. For his logic was not like the logic of the white man. His captives were not only his prisoners but at the same time his guests and their beliefs were to be respected. Respect for the Gods of strangers! Like all early and primitive people this was one of the strongest traits with which they were imbued for one never knew too much about the powers of these foreign spirits. That night he had witnessed something which could not be explained by any Indian lore he had ever heard. If he were to anger the Great Father of whom the man had spoken He might severely punish him. On the other hand were He to be

appeased on this so special night and the
night of His Son He might even sometime
extend His own protection to Quanta.

And so Quanta-wa-neh reached his decision. To slay the captives after what had
taken place would be neither meet nor polite
in terms of the Indian concept of hospitality
to strangers who had pleased them with a
mysterious story nor politic to all Gods. Yes,
even the Great Hare might be offended. "Release them," he ordered. "We will let them
go."

To his command he gave a practical ex-
planation. He said, "You have heard. The
pursuers are too many for us and their ap-

proach rapid. If they find the captives dead they will continue on to take their revenge upon us. But if they come upon them still alive and in need of aid they will stop in the manner of the white man to look after them and will not follow after us. Obey."

And so, Quanta-wa-neh, the savage Algonkin chieftain, gave Jasper and Dorcas and the babe, Asher, their liberty as a Christmas present, but it was Nyagway, the fat, wheezy old Seneca renegade, who out of gratitude made them the gift of life.

Obeying Quanta's instructions the raiding party quickly freed the captives of their bonds, propped them up against the trunk of one of the aged oaks, looked to their weapons, disposed themselves for swift passage and then, like ghosts, vanished northwards once more into the darkness.

But Nyagway waited behind for a moment even though it would cost him much breathlessness and effort to catch up for he knew that he had acquired great merit that night amongst the Algonkin and that the tale that he had told would travel to campfires the length and breadth of the country. No longer would he be known as "The-Foolish-One-Who-Waddles-Like-A-Bear," but instead as "Teller-Of-The-Great-Tale-At-Midnight." And he would be importuned to repeat it in lodge or wigwam. He fumbled at his pouch for a moment, then going to Jasper pressed flint and steel into his hand. Then, without a word, he turned and scuttled off.

Once more Jasper Adams found some last reserve of strength for fire meant warmth and warmth in the winter wilderness was life. He dug into the snow to collect twigs and branches, then crawled painfully to gather spruce boughs for a bed for the child. The sparks from the steel caught his tinder and when the blaze was roaring and the baby warmly bedded he at last allowed himself to rest braced against a tree with his wife held in his arms. Then there came upon him the overwhelming fear that Dorcas might not live through the night for she seemed far gone. Her lips moved and when he bent his head he heard her whisper the prayer of the deer, "Oh Almighty Father and gentle Jesus, let Thy grace descend upon us so that we may live together in peace and love one another."

It was Christmas morning though the dawn had yet to break through the darkness. Jasper looked up into the sky through a giant fir, its branches illuminated as by the candles of the stars that studded the bow of the sky and seemed to lean down and rest upon the needled limbs. And at the very peak of the tree one such star seemed to be affixed there, gleaming blue-white as bright perhaps as that strange one that had appeared over Bethlehem so long ago.

Then for the first and last time in his life Jasper Adams beseeched of his God something for himself.

"Lord God," he prayed, "forgive me for asking yet more of Thee who hast been so merciful to us on this day but what availeth the life Thou hast restoreth to me if Thou takest from me this woman who is my heart and my soul. Spare her, Lord. . . ."

It was not long after this that there came the sound of horses, a jingling of weapons and accouterments and a crashing of many men bursting through the forest aisles and it was thus that the rescue party of Iroquois and British soldiery found them, the man and the woman still alive, the child Asher, on his bed of boughs, awake and laughing at the dancing tongues of fire, orange and red against the snow.

This is how I remember the story as it was told to me by my great-grandmother on the eve of another Christmas by the candlelit tree and the fireside when I was young. . . .